Kieran Greene

Dr. Seuss on the Loose!

It's Fun to Have Fun

"Look at me! Look at me!
Look at me NOW!
It is fun to have fun
But you have to know how.
I can hold up the cup
And the milk and the cake!
I can hold up these books!
And the fish on a rake!
I can hold the toy ship
And a little toy man!
And look! With my tail
I can hold a red fan!
I can fan with the fan
As I hop on the ball!
But that is not all.
Oh, no. That is not all…"

– The Cat in the Hat

Thinks to Think About

You can think up some birds.
That's what you can do.
You can think about yellow
Or think about blue.
You can think about red.
You can think about pink.
You can think up a horse.
Oh, the THINKS you can think!

– Oh the Thinks You Can Think!

How to Tell a Klotz From a Glotz

Well, the Glotz, you will notice,
Has lots of black spots.
The Klotz is quite different
With lots of black dots.
But the big problem is
That the spots on a Glotz
Are about the same size
As the dots on a Klotz.
So you first have to spot
Who the one with the dots is.
Then it's easy to tell
Who the Klotz or the Glotz is.

– *Oh Say Can You Say?*

On Eating Green Eggs and Ham

I would not, could not, in a box.
I could not, would not, with a fox.
I will not eat them with a mouse.
I will not eat them in a house.
I will not eat them here or there.
I will not eat them anywhere.
I do not eat green eggs and ham.
I do not like them, Sam-I-am.

– *Green Eggs and Ham*

The Truffula Trees

Way back in the days when the grass was still green
and the pond was still wet
and the clouds were still clean,
and the song of the Swomee-Swans rang out in space...
one morning, I came to this glorious place.
And I first saw the trees!
The Truffula Trees!
The bright-coloured tufts of the Truffula Trees!
Mile after mile in the fresh morning breeze.

– The Lorax

ONCE-LER
WAGON

Two Vrooms Sweep Clean

Oh, the things you can find if you don't stay behind!
On a world near the sun live two brothers called Vrooms
Who, strangely enough, are built sort of like brooms
And they're stuck all alone up there high in the blue
And so, to kill time, just for something to do
Each one of these fellows takes turn with the other
In sweeping the dust off his world with his brother.

– On Beyond Zebra

Tricks with Bricks and Chicks

And here's a
new trick, Mr. Knox…
Socks on chicks
and chicks on fox.
Fox on clocks
on bricks and blocks.
Bricks and blocks
on Knox on Box.

– *Fox in Socks*

A Person's a Person. No Matter How Small

Through the high jungle tree tops, the news quickly spread:
"He talks to a dust speck! He's out of his head!
Just look at him walk with that speck on that flower!"
And Horton walked, worrying, almost an hour.
"Should I put this speck down?…" Horton thought with alarm.
"If I do, these small persons may come to great harm.
I *can't* put it down. And I *won't!* After all
A person's a person. No matter how small."

– *Horton Hears a Who!*

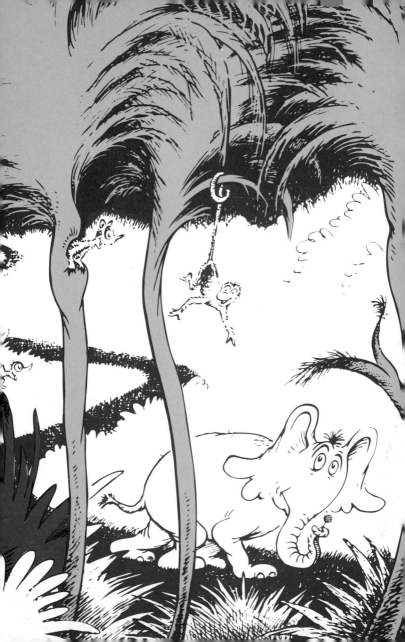

Just Waiting...

Waiting for a train to go
or a bus to come, or a plane to go
or the mail to come, or the rain to go
or the phone to ring, or the snow to snow
or waiting around for a Yes or No
or waiting for their hair to grow.
Everyone is just waiting.

Waiting for the fish to bite
or waiting for wind to fly a kite
or waiting around for Friday night
or waiting, perhaps, for their Uncle Jake
or a pot to boil, or a Better Break
or a string of pearls, or a pair of pants
or a wig with curls, or Another Chance.
Everyone is just waiting.

– Oh, The Places You'll Go!

Perfect Pets

I do not like this one so well.
All he does is yell, yell, yell.
I will not have this one about.
When he comes in I put him out.

This one is quiet as a mouse.
I like to have him in the house.

— *One Fish, Two Fish
Red Fish, Blue Fish*

The Letter O

O is very useful.
You use it when you say:
"Oscar's only ostrich
oiled an orange owl today."

– Dr. Seuss' ABC

Battling Beetles
in a Bottle

When beetles fight these battles
in a bottle with their paddles
and the bottle's on a poodle
and the poodle's eating noodles…

...they call this
a muddle puddle tweetle poodle
beetle noodle bottle paddle battle.

– *Fox in Socks*

Taming the Beast

And now *Here*!
In this cage
Is a beast most ferocious
Who's known far and wide
As the Spotted Atrocious
Who growls, howls and yowls
The most bloodcurdling sounds
And each tooth in his mouth
Weighs at least sixty pounds
And he chews up and eats with the greatest of ease
Things like carpets and sidewalks and people and trees!
But the great Colonel Sneelock is just the right kind
Of a man who can tame him. I'm sure he won't mind.

– If I Ran the Circus

Taking Time Out

Do you know where I found him?
You know where he was?
He was eating a cake in the tub!
Yes he was!
The hot water was on
And the cold water, too.
And I said to the cat,
"What a bad thing to do!"
"But I like to eat cake
In a tub," laughed the cat.
"You should try it some time,"
Laughed the cat as he sat.

– *The Cat in the Hat Comes Back*

Just Bobbing Along

FLOOB is for Floob-Boober-Bab-Boober-Bubs
Who bounce in the water like blubbery tubs.
They're no good to eat.
You can't cook 'em like steaks.
But they're handy in crossing small oceans and lakes.

– *On Beyond Zebra*

There is Fun to be Done!

Oh, the places you'll go! There is fun to be done!
There are points to be scored. There are games to be won.
And the magical things you can do with that ball
will make you the winning-est winner of all.
Fame! You'll be famous as famous can be,
with the whole wide world watching you win on TV.

– Oh, The Places You'll Go!

Time for Bed

Creatures are starting to think about rest.
Two Biffer-Baum Birds are now building their nest.
They do it each night. And quite often I wonder
How they do this big job without making a blunder.
But that is *their* problem.
Not yours. And not mine.
The point is: They're going to bed.
And that's fine.

– Dr. Seuss's Sleep Book

Good Night

And now
good night.
It is time to sleep.
So we will sleep
with our pet Zeep.

Today is gone. Today was fun.
Tomorrow is another one.
Every day,
from here to there,
funny things are everywhere.

– *One Fish, Two Fish, Red Fish, Blue Fish*

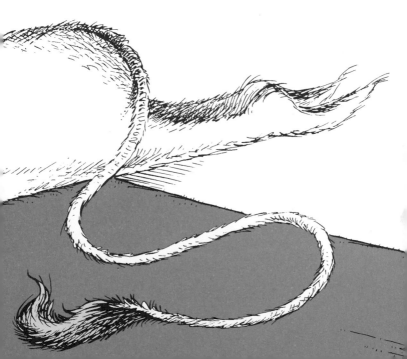

Published specially for World Book Day 2011

First published in paperback in Great Britain in 2011 by HarperCollins*Children's Books,* a division of HarperCollins*Publishers* Ltd

Dr. Seuss on the Loose!
™ & © 2001 by Dr. Seuss Enterprises, L.P.
All Rights Reserved
Original titles published by arrangement with Random House Inc., New York, USA

The HarperCollins website address is:
www.harpercollins.co.uk

ISBN: 978-0-00-741438-3
ISBN: 978-0-00-742558-7 (export edition)

Printed and bound in China

2 4 6 8 10 9 7 5 3 1

Discover the books
that inspired the new
Cat in the Hat TV series

The Cat in the Hat's Learning Library
Lots of subjects, lots of fun!

Celebrate reading with the essential Dr. Seuss collection!

These classic titles are now available in picture book format to welcome a whole new generation to the wonders of Dr. Seuss.

Oh, The Places You'll Go!
PB • 978-0-00-741357-7
PB+CD • 978-0-00-741358-4

In this classic tale, Dr. Seuss primes his readers against all the little mishaps and misadventures that can befall even the best of us!

The Cat in the Hat Comes Back
PB • 978-0-00-735555-6
PB+CD • 978-0-00-735554-9

The sequel to the world famous 'The Cat in the Hat' is a must-have for any Dr. Seuss fan!

The Cat in the Hat
PB • 978-0-00-734869-5
PB+CD • 978-0-00-734745-2

Green Eggs and Ham
PB • 978-0-00-735591-4
PB+CD • 978-0-00-735592-1

How the Grinch Stole Christmas!
PB • 978-0-00-736554-8
PB+CD • 978-0-00-736555-5